This book is for

IRVING CHASE SHELDON

master of *Wings*, fulminator,
keen critic, and dear friend

# W O R K

Copyright 2004 by Jan Adkins

Published by WoodenBoat Publications Inc
Naskeag Road, PO Box 78
Brooklin, Maine 04616 USA
www.woodenboat.com

ISBN: 0-937822-80-9

Originally published by Charles Scribner & Sons, 1985

Written and illustrated by Jan Adkins
Printed in Canada by Friesens

# B O A T S

written & illustrated by Jan Adkins

WoodenBoat Books, Brooklin, Maine

I want to write a truthful book about men and women and the sea. You and I have read books about pirates and treasure galleons, about hunting the great white whale, and about uncharted islands full of jungles and jewels. There must have been some truth in all of that, but not now. The big sailing ships are gone, and the islands all have names.

While we are reading this book, though, stubborn, powerful little motor vessels are working through storms and feeling their way through fog and the dark to bring back fish, move cargo, and carry passengers. In the same storms and fogs the Coast Guard works day and night to keep them all safe.

The people on the boats live in the weather, become a part of it. You and I, living on land, run from the bus to the doorway under an umbrella. Their hands are cold, sometimes. Sometimes they are tired, and sick, and scared. They ship out again, though, because their life on the water is big and strong and beautiful. Only a quarter of the world's surface is land; the rest is theirs.

Many of the people in this book are real. The places are real: Buzzards Bay and Vineyard Sound and Cape Cod are in Massachusetts. The most truthful parts of the book are the boats and the common, everyday courage of the people on them.

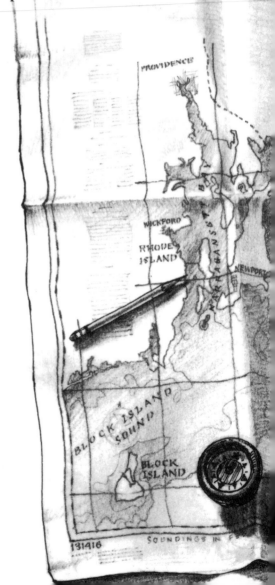

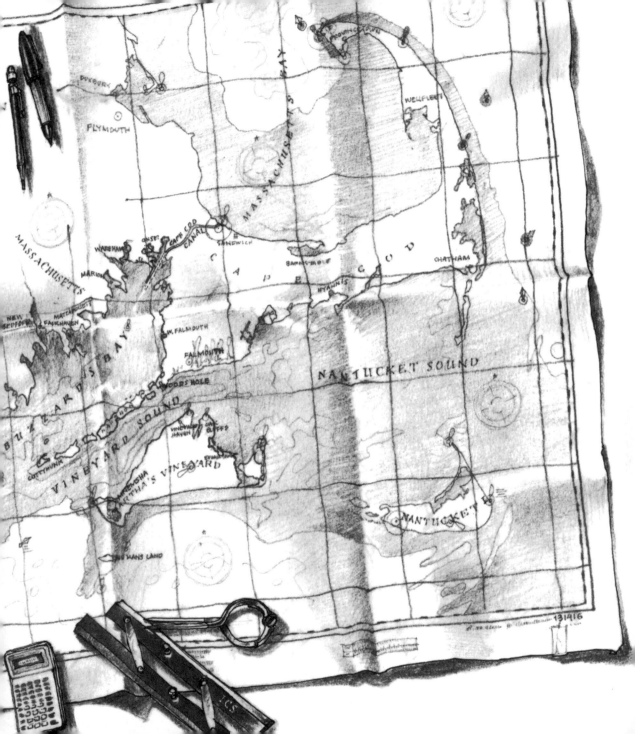

At sunset Buzzards Bay was quiet. The boats in Wareham Harbor drifted gently around their anchors. But a storm was coming. At midnight a blanket of damp air slid over the Berkshire Mountains, thunderstorms grumbling along its edge, and by morning the boats were swinging back and forth, straining against their lines like frightened horses.

Skip Warr knew it would be a long day. He came down to the float at six to check the lines of the dinghies and dories and prams. They are the small change of the harbor, scurrying between shore and the bigger boats anchored out in deep water.

Two dinghies were chewing at the motorboat float as the wind nudged them against it. He moved them around to the side away from the wind. No one would take small motorboats out today, not for fun. Only the workboats would be on the Bay today.

Skip dropped down into the Warr's Marine Railway yard boat, an old bass boat with a big inboard engine and no name. It started with a rumble. He cast off the lines and motored out into the harbor.

8 foot PRAM

"painter" for tying up

Oarlock holds oar for rowing

Bailer scoops out water

10 foot SKIFF

light

gas tank

Well for outboard motor

17 foot BOSTON WHALER

post for towing

engine

23 foot inboard runabout YARD BOAT

controls

bumper

fiberglass dinghy

wooden skiff

plastic dinghy

laminated wood peapod

inflatable dinghy

He nosed the yard boat up the Wareham River to the Narrows Cafe. He spun it around in the current rushing out through the pilings of the bridges—the tide was going out—and tied up to the float beside Rob Sheldon's quahog skiff. Inside, Rob sat at the counter eating eggs, waiting for low tide.

Quahogs are hard-shell clams. When they're small they're called cherrystones or littlenecks. Folks eat them raw with hot sauce. When they grow big and tough they're ground for chowder or for quahog pancakes. You've got to be a real Yankee to like the pancakes.

Pulling the thirty-foot handle of the quahog rake, straining the Bay's bottom mud for "hogs," has given Rob the shoulders and arms of a weight lifter. Skip ordered pie. He asked Rob if he had seen Peter Farrel. His mouth full, Rob shook his head. No, he hadn't.

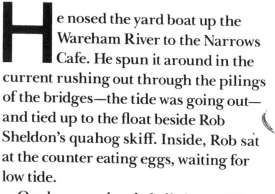

*twine net bag*

*frame & blade*

*chain bag bottom*

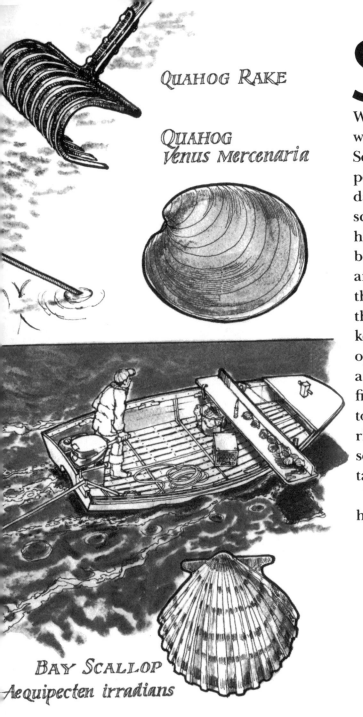

QUAHOG RAKE

QUAHOG
Venus Mercenaria

BAY SCALLOP
Aequipecten irradians

S kip was worried. Peter's boat was missing from the anchorage, but his car was in the parking lot. Where could he be, with a storm on its way? Peter was a teacher at Sippican School who tended about ten lobster pots from his Whaler. In these early fall days he rigged his boat to drag for Bay scallops. With his outboard motor slow he towed the scallop dredge across the bottom, where its blade scraped them up and held them in its net. He would dump them onto a sorting board and open them up with a round-ended knife, keeping the tiny, tasty muscle that opened and closed their delicate shells, and tossing the rest back to the Bay. The fish market bought some, and some he took home to his family. Quahogs taste rich and strong, like the bottom, but scallops, fried in butter or broiled, taste like a sweet, warm wind.

The wind was chill this morning, and harsh. Skip worried about his friend.

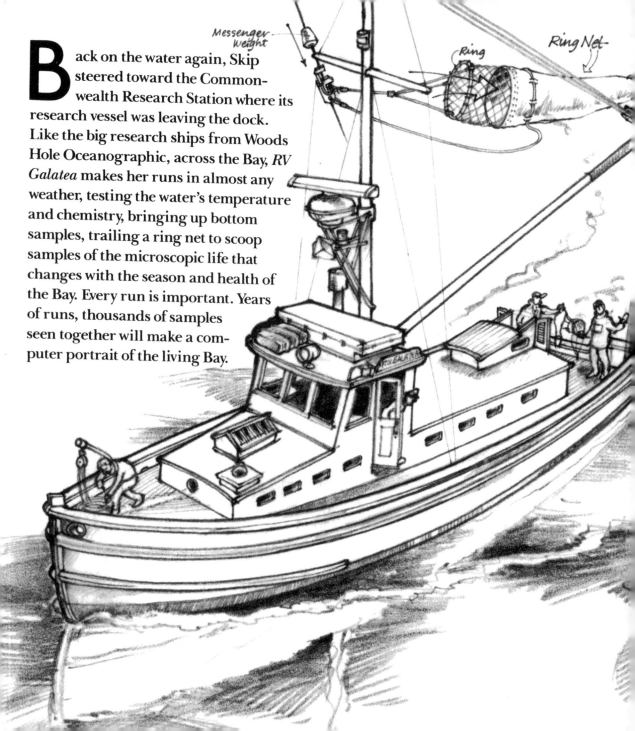

**B**ack on the water again, Skip steered toward the Commonwealth Research Station where its research vessel was leaving the dock. Like the big research ships from Woods Hole Oceanographic, across the Bay, *RV Galatea* makes her runs in almost any weather, testing the water's temperature and chemistry, bringing up bottom samples, trailing a ring net to scoop samples of the microscopic life that changes with the season and health of the Bay. Every run is important. Years of runs, thousands of samples seen together will make a computer portrait of the living Bay.

Messenger Weight

Ring

Ring Net

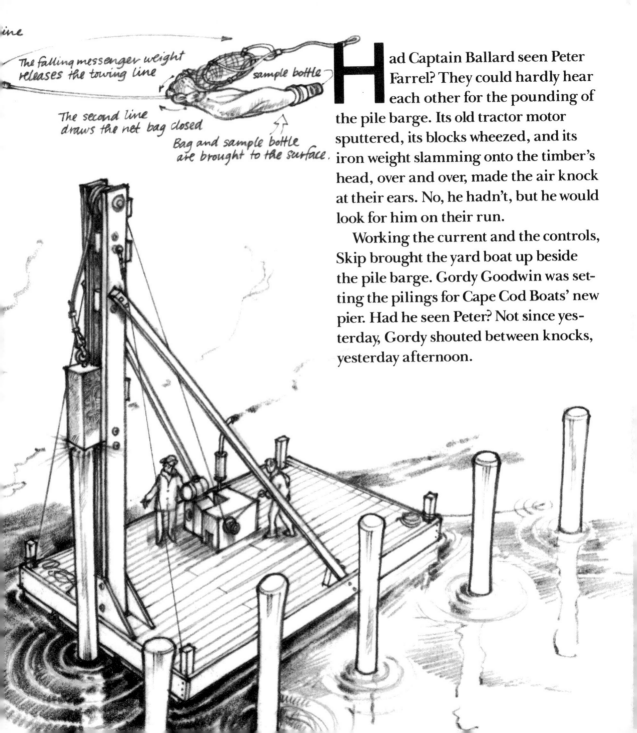

The falling messenger weight releases the towing line

sample bottle

The second line draws the net bag closed

Bag and sample bottle are brought to the surface.

H ad Captain Ballard seen Peter Farrel? They could hardly hear each other for the pounding of the pile barge. Its old tractor motor sputtered, its blocks wheezed, and its iron weight slamming onto the timber's head, over and over, made the air knock at their ears. No, he hadn't, but he would look for him on their run.

Working the current and the controls, Skip brought the yard boat up beside the pile barge. Gordy Goodwin was setting the pilings for Cape Cod Boats' new pier. Had he seen Peter? Not since yesterday, Gordy shouted between knocks, yesterday afternoon.

At Skip's dock Carl Taylor was loading a barrel of lobster bait, week-old flounder backs from the filet factories in New Bedford. If you tell a lobsterman his bait stinks he will grin enthusiastically and nod, Yup, it sure does, it's a good barrel. It's the smell of the rotting fish underwater that brings the lobsters across the bottom to the pots. They crawl in through the funnel-shaped head net and can't get out.

But lobsters eat anything: old flounder backs, each other. To protect his catch the lobsterman must pull his pots every two or three days. Each lobsterman's buoys have their own colors and design. Even in the fog, using his compass, the way the waves change with the bottom, the direction birds fly to and from their nesting places, Carl finds the strings of buoys he has laid down over the rock piles and ridges of the bottom. He plucks up a buoy, flips its line over a hanging block, and hauls it up with a power winch. His lobsterboat is steady, quick-turning, fast but economical to run, a specialized workboat that has been used for fifty years or more. It is the tool he uses to know the Bay and where the lobsters are, to make his living. He knows the Bay as much as any waterman but he has not seen Peter.

toggle buoy keeps line from chafing on the bottom

Rocky bottom where lobsters hide

LOBSTER POT    bait inside.

head net

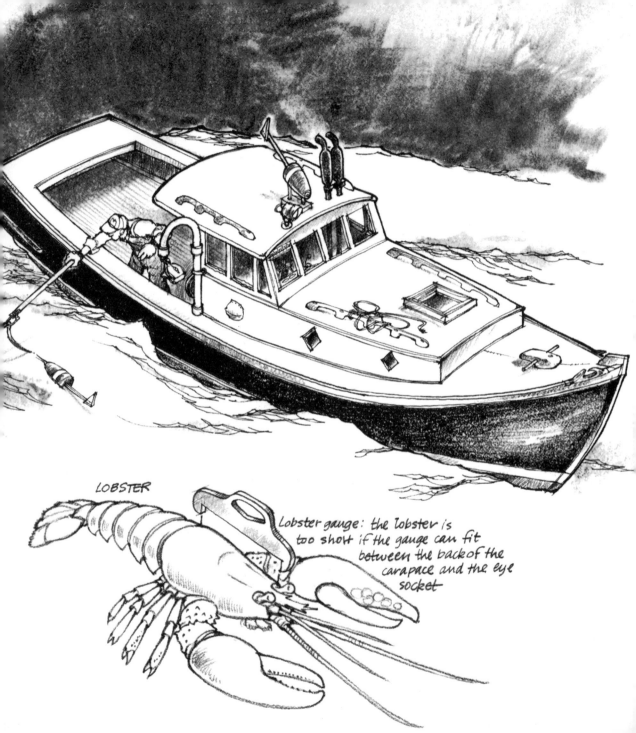

LOBSTER

Lobster gauge: the lobster is too short if the gauge can fit between the back of the carapace and the eye socket

Static hissed and crackled from the speaker: Skip's radio heard lightning in the storm front on its way. If Peter had motored through Woods Hole on his way to Martha's Vineyard one of the ferry crew might have seen him.

Along any broken coast, where there are island towns and villages, there are ferries. The big ferries out of Woods Hole are built to carry people, cars, and trucks. The Islands depend on them, life in the villages around their docks is timed to their arrivals and departures. Their high sides are buttoned up crossing the choppy Sounds. Their radar reaches through the weather for buoys and the shape of the land, their depth sounders reach for the bottom below them. They churn the water around their dock ramps into a pale foam as their propellors ease them slowly into place. Lines are thrown and made fast, and they open their great steel mouths to give out food, supplies, medicine, fuel, and—most important for Martha's Vineyard and Nantucket—tourists. They are steady, safe, and reliable in anything short of a hurricane.

Skip switched to the channel used by the ferries. Across the Bay he described Peter and his boat, and asked Captain Stackpole of the *Islander* if he had seen this fellow. No luck. He called the little *Alert* that serves Cuttyhunk from New Bedford. Nothing. He got Captain Holzer of the freight ferry *Auriga*: "What are conditions down your way?" "For us, not too bad, Skip, but awful for a little boat."

MV **NAUSHON**

MV **ISLANDER**

MV **UNCATENA**

MV **NANTUCKET**

MV **AURIGA**
FREIGHT BOAT

The Coast Guard Buoy Tender *Bittersweet* heard Skip on the calling channel. *Bittersweet* was returning to her station in Woods Hole; it was much too rough for her work, now, perhaps the most dangerous of the Guard's many chores.

On the heaving, breaking surface of the water there is no easy path; one wave looks like another. Buoys are the only street signs. Their numbers and shapes, colors, sounds, and lights say to the sailor, Here is a place on the Bay and on the chart, and there is a way to the next buoy. *Bittersweet* sets the buoys in their exact places, checks them, replaces them when they are shifted by ice or their lights give out or rust breaks through their paint or weeds beard thick around them. Her deck crane lifts a steel buoy and its thick steel chain and the concrete "sinker" that anchors it to the bottom. Tons of gear swing and turn with every wave. The men and women on deck move carefully, respectfully.

The radio operator answered Skip, no sight of the boat. If Peter was near a buoy, though, he would know where he was: *Bittersweet* had done her job.

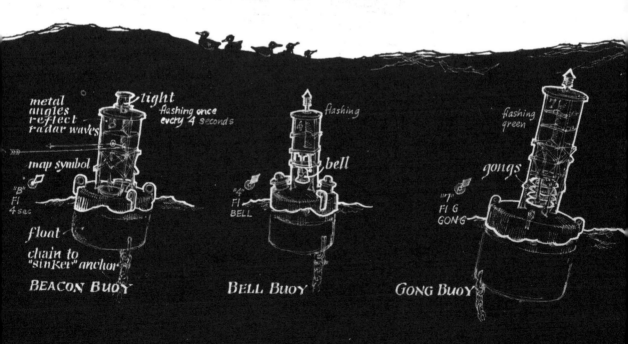

metal angles reflect radar waves

light

flashing once every 4 seconds

map symbol

"B" Fl 4 sec

float

chain to "sinker" anchor

BEACON BUOY

flashing

bell

"A" Fl BELL

BELL BUOY

flashing green

gongs

"7" Fl G GONG

GONG BUOY

544

COAST GUARD

C "3"

N "6"

CAN

NUN

Farther down Vineyard Sound a swordfisherman heard the call. Bunkie Adams had his hands full but he reported in: he hadn't seen Peter, either. His boat was making heavy way against big seas, but he knew he would be safe in Mnemsha Pond soon; it was Steve, above him, who was in trouble.

They had been offshore. Steve Sperry circled in his airplane, looking for the shapes of swordfish basking at the surface, directing the boat to them as Bunkie watched from the high mast hoops. The swordfish is afraid of nothing; it is the fastest fish in the sea and nearly the most powerful. Bunkie balanced on the end of his boat's long pulpit and raised the harpoon, his mate Tom guided the boat on the sharp fin, and just before Bunkie drove his dart in, the fish's wide, cold eye swiveled up in cold anger. The barrel float was thrown overboard; the fish fought against it until its strength was gone. Then the buoy was hauled in, and with it the swordfish, defeated.

The seas were big, like moving hills, but boats are built for the sea. It was Steve's landing in the heavy wind that worried Bunkie.

the dart

At midmorning the storm was blowing itself out. *Judy G.*, a small gillnetter out of Block Island, was trailing out her last line of net. Michael Galavotti, her skipper, would be glad to head home. Setting the gear in heavy swells was punishing work for Michael and his three sons. They had dropped the ground tackle, a large anchor, for one end; its float and flag buoy bobbed and waved two hundred yards behind them. Now the length of net paid out and arranged itself like an underwater fence; lead weights pressed its hem against the bottom, a necklace of buoys held it up, and the ground tackle at both ends would keep it taut. Small schools of fish would pass through the mesh, big stripers and sharks would be turned aside, but fish of

flag

anchor

floats

the right market size—Michael was planning on a fat school of cod, perhaps some haddock—would be caught in the net, locked in by the forward slant of their gills. Tomorrow or the next day *Judy G.* would return and run slowly along the string while the net was winched in over her side and the catch was separated and sorted.

There, it was set, now for home. He read the sea, working the throttle and the wheel to ease *Judy G.* over the crests and bring her up out of the troughs. Bobby came into the deck house as the alert for Peter Farrel was broadcast again. Could it have been a half-sunk Whaler they had seen off Westport, close inshore? Michael nodded; it was worth a call.

*the Atlantic Cod*

t's not the ocean that's dangerous, Captain Gomez told Joann at the wheel. It's the hard stuff around the edges. The *Eagle* was dragging for flounder on the Nantucket Shoals. Lines stretched out from her stern to the otter doors that strained outward like underwater kites, keeping the mouth of the trawl net open. Soon they would slow down and begin hauling the net: the wings, then the belly would be reeled in over the stern, but the cod end that held the catch would be lifted up over the deck. A good deckhand would approach the dripping, swinging net like a lion tamer, confident but tense, and would untie the cod-end knot. With a sudden, silvery rush the catch spills out, a flipping, living mound of sea robins, skates, dogfish sharks, strange, beautiful

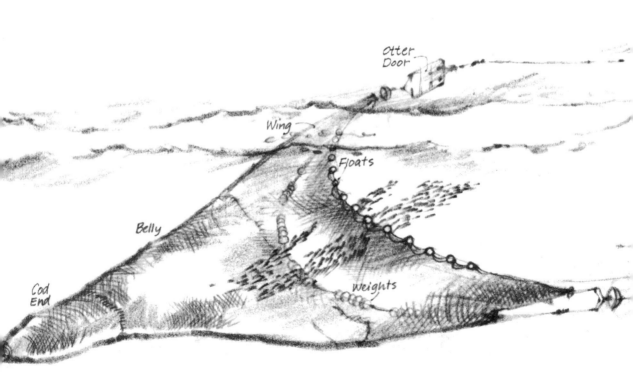

things, with the delicious, valuable flounder. The hands wade through them in their high boots, balancing on the fish-slippery deck, sorting the catch into deck chutes with blunt-tined pitchforks.

Gomez heard the alert. No small boat will be out here, he thought, but I wish him well wherever he is.

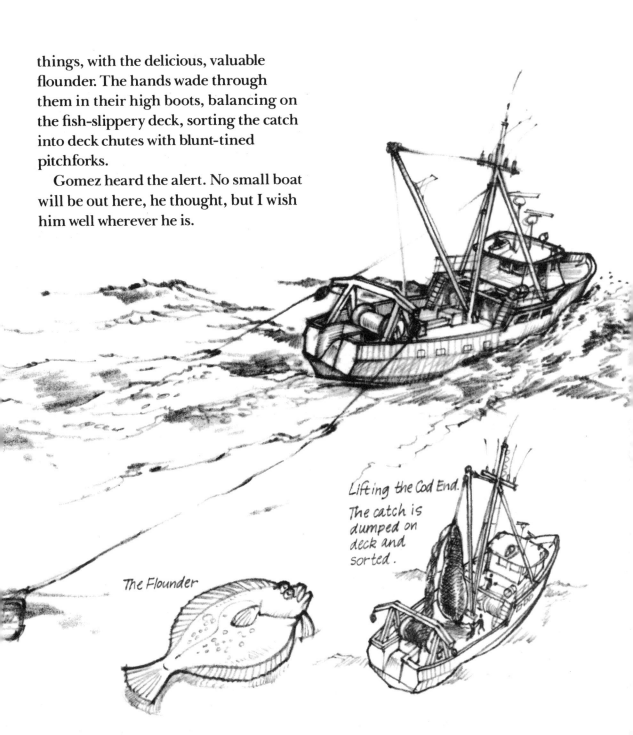

The Flounder

Lifting the Cod End.
The catch is dumped on deck and sorted.

id-day. The storm was easing and the solid sky was breaking into individual clouds that fled toward the open sea. The big white helicopter tore at the unsteady air as the Elizabeth Islands slid below it, a rough ride: Naushon, Uncatena, and Nonamesset, the tiny Weepeckets, Pasque, Nashawena, stubborn Cuttyhunk, lonely Penikese, then the width of the Bay. Its pilot changed the pitch and throttled the jet turbines back to approach the mainland lower and slower. They swept along the rocky coast to the Westport River. There it was in the shallows, an abandoned boat. They circled, looking

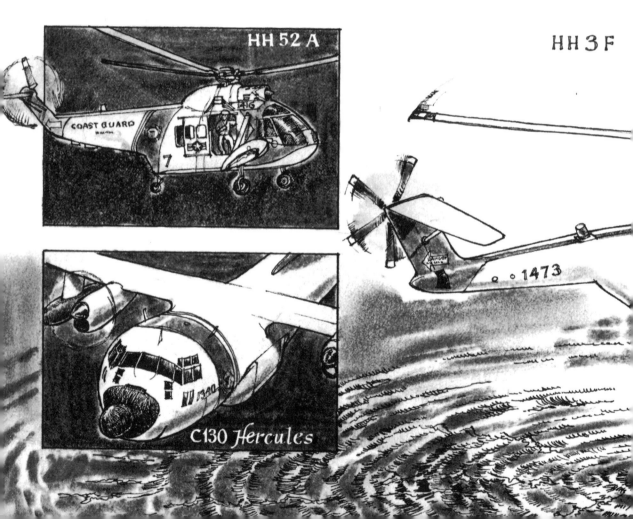

HH 52 A

COAST GUARD

7

HH 3 F

1473

C130 Hercules

for something else in the water, hoping not to find it. Nothing. With difficulty the pilot held the big machine over the boat. The co-pilot called their base. The missing boat, was it a seventeen footer with a center console? Yes. Negative; this is a thirteen with a frayed mooring line, just a runaway. Notify the harbormaster at Westport. Returning to base.

Coming up the coast a huge Coast Guard C-130 supply plane heard the call and requested a lower altitude to aid the search. Another helicopter off Chatham altered course and flew the eastern shore of the Bay, searching.

Tugboats may lack grace but they make it up in style, an unmistakeable jauntiness. They are all muscle, little more than hulls and housings for big engines, snub-nosed and long-flanked, hung with tattered truck tires and pinned with bitts that make fast anaconda-thick lines for towing. They come in all sizes: little harbor tugs, the toughs of the waterfront; ship-docking tugs that work in pairs and trios to berth and bring out tankers and freighters and, still, the occasional luxury liner; coastwise tugs that tow barges of oil, cement, grain, coal, and ore; deep-sea tugs that bring disabled ships back to port.

The *Miriam* was bringing a barge south through the Cape Cod Canal. Jake Tibbets, her captain, had been listening to the search reports and alerts all morning. He had caught the last of a fair current through the canal, steering delicately between the stone-lined banks, and had cleared the Onset end in the mid-afternoon. As he neared the long sand spit that protects the canal channel on the Buzzards Bay side he glanced into The Widow's Cove from his high pilot house. What was that in the marsh? Even a tug can't stop 40,000 barrels of oil inside half a mile; he motored on but called the Coast Guard immediately.

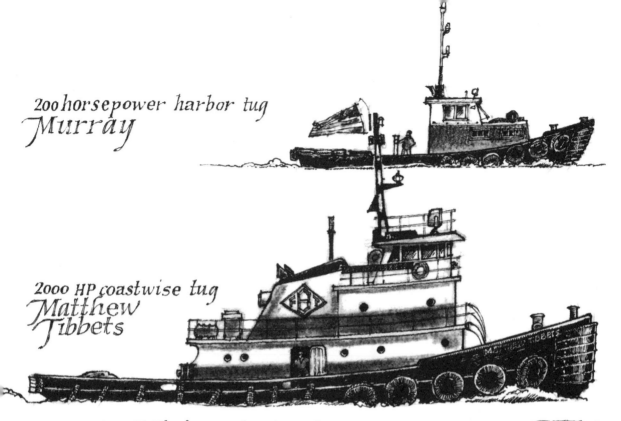

200 horsepower harbor tug
*Murray*

2000 HP coastwise tug
*Matthew Tibbets*

1600 HP tug *Miriam* towing the 40,000-barrel oil barge *BFT 39*

It was a wide net but the catch had been poor. Coast Guard vessels from Provincetown to Block Island were searching for a seventeen-foot outboard and a schoolteacher from Marion. It is their job, they make the water a safer place to fish, carry goods, explore, even have fun. It is a serious, exciting job they do well.

Commander Linda Brown, skipper of the *Vigilant* on Drug Interdiction Patrol, brought her cutter inside the Buzzards Bay Entrance Light Tower to make a search sweep.

The eighty-two foot *Point Heron* made a run along the northern side of the Vineyard, just in case.

The forty-four foot steel patrol boat is one of the Coast Guard's sturdiest workhorses. When the tug captain's call came

44' Steel Launch

82' Launch

210' Medium Endurance Cutter *Vigilant*

COAST GUARD    617

through, Seaman Andy Walker was bringing a patrol boat through Woods Hole. He passed the entrance to the Coast Guard Station and took his boat up Broadway and into The Strait. He gave number three, the black can at the turn, plenty of room as it swung dangerously in the fierce current but was careful not to be set onto the rocks of Devil's Foot Island. Woods Hole is always a serious business.

Safely in Buzzards Bay, Seaman Walker reported to his base. "I know that cove, but we can't get in with our boat. The water's thin and full of bricks. Someone with a shallow-draft boat and local knowledge will have to get up in there."

S kip had been working near the radio all day listening to the search. Now he had something to go on. He knew The Widow's Cove, and the voice on the radio was right: it was shallow and full of rocks; getting in would take someone who knew the shore as Carl Taylor and the other lobstermen knew the bottom. Studley, the shellfish warden; he knew every clamming and quahogging flat on the Bay and he lived just around the point from the Cove in Onset. Skip picked up the telephone.

The clouds were breaking up and there were patches of blue sky. Studley pulled down his cap more tightly as he rounded the point in his shallow draft runabout. He could see a Coast Guard patrol boat passing the end of the sand spit.

Easing past a ledge of sunken rocks Studley could see how an injured man might be stuck here. The marsh was surrounded by thick brush and woods. He brought his boat around a tuft of high reeds, turned up into the marsh, and found Peter Farrel.

Studley set his anchor and hurried across the sand. The Whaler was beached. Peter was sitting wearily on the bow with his arm slung up in a bandanna. "Peter," Studley called, "you all right?"

"Considering the alternative," Peter said, "I'm fine as kind, and I am glad to see you, Studley." He winced as he held out his hand.

A big patch of blue opened up as Studley brought Peter across the cove, trailing the Whaler. The late sun lit up Skip's red jeep on the Burgess Point side. Skip and Dr. Finn were waiting on the shore. The Coast Guard patrol boat let out a happy yelp with its horn.

They bundled Peter up and helped him into the jeep. Peter's propellor had hit a rock and he had been thrown against the side of the boat. The tide had taken him deeper into the Cove.

Only when the Whaler was safely towed out of The Widow's Cove did the red jeep leave for Tobey Hospital. The white patrol boat waited, too, then spun in the current and started down Buzzards Bay. It had other work to do.

# Acknowledgments

Writing any book is a painful exposure of the author's ignorance that comes perilously close to outright lying. No writer could risk such foolishness without the help of friends. I thank them all. John Swain Carter, old friend and director of the Maine Maritime Museum, was and is important. Marine architect John W. Gilbert and tugboatman Jake Tibbets have been patient and helpful. Marine writer Jim Gibson has lent his advice. The Fish and Wildlife Service risked a rare last copy of a crucial circular. Photos have been kindly lent by The Woods Hole, Martha's Vineyard and Nantucket Steamship Authority, George Bartholomew *(RV Galatea)*, and Mullen Advertising, Inc. (Boston Whalers). The United States Coast Guard has been remarkably responsive and pleasant, and I send a special salute to *USCGC Eagle's* Captain Ernst Cummings. Affectionate thanks to type mavens Charles Uhl and John Grandits, who consulted on design, and to my great teacher Howard Paine, from whom I have much to learn. My love and thanks to my wife, Dorcas, and to my children, Sally, Robbie, and Sam, who are the ribs and hull of my life.

The copy for this book was composed on a Columbia computer using Perfect Writer software. The drawings were made with technical pens and fibre-tips with charcoal and graphite shading on Strathmore drawing paper and tracing vellum. The text type is ITC Baskerville Semibold, set by Cardinal Type Service.